Ghost Walk

Native American
Tales of the Spirit

IRIE BOOKS
Pine Island, Florida

This was book was originally published by Mariposa Printing
and Publishing in Santa Fe, New Mexico in 1991. There were
three paperback printings altogether. This is the first
Irie Books edition. The story *Pale Ghost* appeared in
Phantoms of the Night edited by Richard Gilliam and
Martin H. Greenberg, published by DAW Books.

For more information: Irie Books, 12699 Cristi Way,
Bokeelia, Florida 33922 USA

ISBN 0-9709112-3-8
10 9 8 7 6 5 4 3 2
Printed in China.

Ghost Walk

Native American
Tales of the Spirit

GERALD HAUSMAN

DRAWINGS BY
SID HAUSMAN

TABLE OF CONTENTS

Little Bear Canyon

oren hiked into the Gila on a full moon night in August. The switchbacks where they cut into the canyon wound four miles down to the basin where the Little Bear River ran between the vertical walls of stone. He walked until there was no more trail. Then in the light of the moon, Loren spread his nylon poncho on the dry sand.

On the canyon's rim, the bear's head stood out against the pale sky. The rock-topped dome was furry with scrub. The bear's round ears were silvered in the moon.

Loren thought, *there are things that aren't there and things that are…and the canyon has a say in what we see.*

When he was a young boy and his grandfather was alive, the old man told Loren about the canyon. How he'd wandered into it on a trip with some friends. Far away from Navajo land, he found something precious.

Loren remembered his grandfather's face right after that trip. How he was always smiling.

Grandfather never said what it was he'd seen, or what had happened to him, only that he'd washed his hair in the old way. Camped by the river, watched the moon rise in back of the rock top bear on the canyon rim, and then he'd come home with something. A gift from Little Bear Canyon.

Loren fell asleep.

And dreamed.

I see him washing his hair in the old way with yucca root. Pounding the root, scrubbing his hair with thin white suds, pouring cold creek water on his head from an old Army canteen. I see him sitting in the sun, satisfied. Combing his hair with his fingers. He's old but his hair's raven, and black as lightning.

When Loren woke, he felt the warm sun on his eyelids. It was midmorning, maybe ten o'clock. In the cottonwoods on the other side of the river, Loren heard parrots screaming. He chuckled, *tropical birds living in a desert canyon. But I know they come up from Mexico. Grandfather brought one thing back from his trip—a blue green parrot feather.*

Listening to the birds quarreling in the leaves, Loren remembered last night's dream. *I see Grandfather pounding that stubborn yucca root by the river. Then I reach up and feel my own hair, which is matted and stiff from the sweaty hike into the canyon. How strange, I am not yet eighteen*

years of age and my hair is already turning white.
This had started to happen when I was in the
sixth grade. Back then it frightened me. I asked
my mother to dye it black for me, but she says my
hair turning is natural. "Some young men of the
tribe have wise hair," she says. Then she tells me
the legend of Nuthatch. That's the little bird that
sprinkled wisdom dust on the heads of the people.
And so, they got white hair. And the people knew
what it was like to grow old.

In the canyon sitting by the river, Loren
wondered what was true, and what was not.
Things done in the traditional way . . . did they
really bring tradition into a man's life?

Loren had stopped dyeing his hair black. Not just to please his mother. Or because of an old Indian legend. His classmates, some of them, still called him "the old man." Now, listening to the cackles of the parrots, the thought came to him, gently and persuasively. *I see the yucca plant in the loose rock alongside the cliff. I will go up there and dig it out. The loose rock and sandy soil make it easy to find the secret white root.*

The yucca joined him to his grandfather. And the canyon. Soon the yucca was soapy on his hair. Loren put his head into the cold river, and opened his eyes underwater. *The water makes my eyes ache.*

He rubbed on more yucca, and soaped again.

It was late morning by the time Loren's hair was dry in the sun. The noisy parrots went off bickering. The sun was hot. Loren went for a swim, came out refreshed. Then he lay on his back in the sun, and fell asleep. When he woke he knew he hadn't dreamed. His skin, when he touched it, burned. He'd been too long in the sun. There was nothing to do but make supper.

When the sun set on the hair of the bear, Loren realized—*I haven't said a word all day. I*

*wonder if my voice, so long silent, will sound rusty
in the dry air?*

He sang a soft, whisper chant as he fried
bacon in a skillet. And he listened to himself, as
if he were someone else. His little chant and the
rain song of the skillet grease were in harmony.
Loren smiled. *I like being alone. Sometimes you
get lonely, but that's all right. The feeling itself
isn't so bad. It's how you feel about it. That's what
makes you feel weird inside.*

After eating a bacon and egg sandwich, Loren
lay back on his poncho. He listened to the wind
in the cottonwoods. There was a thrumming
noise. The way a single guitar string sounds when
it's plucked. The canyon sighing. Sending out air
at the close of day. In the morning, the wind did
just opposite, sucked air into the canyon. *Like the
breathing of a person. The canyon is a person. A
being, just like Grandfather said.*

When darkness came, the noises of owl and
cricket crept softly into the canyon. Loren rose,
went for a walk. The longer he walked, the more
he felt a yearning--perhaps to find something. A

parrot feather, like his grandfather's, perhaps. He stumbled in the shadows. Halfway up the canyon wall, he asked himself--*why have I come so far?*

Down in the deep canyon's belly, his campfire sent up a ribbon of smoke that mingled with the wind. Loren looked around him. He was in a sheltered place full of stunted oak and gnarled cactus. Little dry leaves were caught in his hair, which he'd bound into a ponytail. He felt the weight of his hair settle between his shoulder blades as he walked steadily upward.

Grandfather is laughing at me now. Look at me—lost.

This made him laugh out loud. The word "lost" sounded funny. He yelled it out into the blue darkness. The empty echo turned round, came back. Loren felt foolish. He sat down on a rock.

Grandfather used to tell me that when I felt lost it was because my mind hadn't caught up with my body. So it's a good thing to sit down.

Loren looked about and saw how thick the undergrowth was. There was nothing familiar about it. After a little while the moon came up

over the rim. He couldn't see it, but he heard the
coyotes talking about it. The canyon brightened
in the moonlight.

Scanning the rocks above, Loren saw an
opening. A dark hole into the otherwise smooth
cliff. Was it big enough for a man to squeeze into?
What was on the other side of it?

Another moment, Loren was at the entrance;
he pulled himself in. Once inside, Loren was
surprised that it wasn't dark, as he'd supposed.
He found himself in a small hollow sheltered by

an overbite of rock. A secret room in an ancient stone house. Hidden away . . . *am I the first person to find it?*

The moonlight lay like snow on the floor of the house. Loren surveyed the silence, broken only by the far away call of a small owl.

Although empty of life, the house did not feel dead. Loren felt awkward. He knelt on the sand floor. A few feet in front of him was a mano and metaté. The cup-shaped stone and grinder used for crushing corn. Loren stood up. Suddenly the hair on his neck stood up with him. He felt something, but he wasn't sure what it was. His presence seemed intrusive. He felt ill at ease.

Then Loren saw loom-ties hanging from the north wall of the room. *Someone, a woman, maybe, strung those ties to the wall so she could weave a blanket.* There were knobs of wood that secured the ties to the stone.

Loren squatted down again.

It was then he felt himself not to be alone.

Someone was nearby, watching.

He was not afraid. Gradually, as he breathed deeply in and out, he sensed it was not an enemy.

Loren glanced about the room. Nothing was there that *could* be there.

Just himself, and this queer feeling of something not-quite-human watching him. He felt it strongly by his right shoulder. It was an old one.

He said into the night, "What do you want, Grandfather?"

Of course he didn't mean *his* grandfather, but the elder whose presence kept shifting about the moonlit room.

A voice broke the silence. "I want to be sure no harm comes to you."

"I am all right sitting here." Loren felt the little hairs on his neck rise again. His voice trembled when he spoke.

"Yes," said the other. "You seem all right."

A long silence.

The voice said, "Do I know you?"

"I don't think so."

"Would you like to have a look at me?"

"Yes."

"Turn around."

A small man with hair cut square below the ears and with bangs in the front of his face, Pueblo style. He was short with the hands of a child. His face was round. He was wearing only a deerskin breechcloth that hung past his knees.

"I see you looking at me," he said. "I am no longer one of the people."

Loren didn't respond.

The man laughed.

"Can you tell that I am not one of the people anymore?"

"Your skin," Loren said, "it's almost clear."

"Can you see all the way through me?"

"Not quite."

"What is it like?"

Loren said, "It's like looking through the rain."
But the moment he said this, he knew it wasn't
right. He could've said the man was made of
moonlight, but that wasn't right either.

"Have a look around," the man said.

Loren nodded. As he glanced about he saw
something he hadn't seen before.

There was a woman kneeling by the loom-ties.
She was grinding corn. A child, close by her, was
playing with a cornhusk doll. Neither one seemed
to notice him. For a moment he felt he was the
ghost and they were the living.

"Do not try to pick up anything that you see
here," the man warned. "Leave the bulrush mats,
the black water jars, the grinding tools. They
belong to us."

Loren said, "I have no desire to touch them."

"Good," the man said. Then he added, "Do
you know why we are here?"

Loren shook his head.

The man came closer to Loren. "Long ago,
he said, "there was a great flood. I was a watcher.
My work was to tell the others when the waters

23

rose halfway up the canyon wall, so we could
move to safety. But I was young, and foolish. The
night I was supposed to be on watch, I was hunting turkey. When I got back to where our village
used to be, the water had carried away everything.
The only family that survived the flood was my
own. There were the three of us left. We stayed
here, alone. I would not forget that I was the one
who had caused this to happen. Because of me,
everyone was gone but us. Time passed. My wife
and child died of old age. I, alone, lived. I was
the last one of our tribe. I lived on. Deer were
plentiful. The cattails by the river grew tall and

sweet. But I was completely alone. Sometimes I saw hunters come into the canyon. But they always went out the way they came. Then I was alone again. The years went by. I grew old and feeble. One day, I died."

The man seemed to be tired of talking.

Loren waited, then asked, "How is it that you seem so . . . young?"

The man said, "I am what you see."

Loren said nothing.

Finally, the other said, "I am a watcher. You were lost, I helped you to see my home."

"I can find my way now," Loren said.

He stood up. The man was gone.

Loren was stiff from sitting still. He gave the empty house a last look. The loom-ties hung in the windless air. He looked for the woman and the child. They weren't there. Nothing was there except what had always been there.

Loren crawled through the hole in the canyon wall. Then he hiked downhill in the moonlight. When he came to the river, there was harmony in his bones and when he got to the box elder tree where his bedroll lay in cold moony silence, he gazed up at the canyon rim. The moon had just found the bear cub.

This meant he'd been gone from the campsite for only a few minutes.

He sat down on his bedroll, let this strange fact seep into his mind.

The box elder bugs began to crawl on his arms and legs. One wandered across his face. He didn't brush it off. He sat quietly attending to the moon as it crossed over the head of the bear cub.

Then he saw the feather.

Stuck in the sand, it stood straight.

A blue-green parrot feather.

Loren rubbed it against his cheek.

Thank you, he said.

Rain Runner

One hour before the 10-kilometer cross-country race, Rain Runner saw the hawk, her brother, fly overhead.

Now, she was running through the middle distance of the race. There were three Ute men and one Navajo just behind her. She didn't know how close they were, but she could hear them breathing in unison.

They were close.

She would not look back to see where they were. This was a race of the heart across country she knew by heart—her own Navajo country. It was an open race for anyone over 18 years of age.

As she ran, even and low, bending into the wind that was coming at her from behind and giving her an edge, she heard her grandmother laugh.

--Ha, ho, ha, ho—

Didn't one of the Hero Twins, sacred deities of the Navajo, children of the Sun Himself, run a race like this? Her grandmother's face flitted across her vision. Yes, it was so . . . the softer brother, the womanlike one known as Born Of Water. He'd been chased by a band of Utes. That was why her grandmother came into it; she'd told Rain this story when she was starting out as a runner.

The Ute braves in back of her did not want to be beaten by a woman. They pressed on, hard. She felt them in the place where fear lived. These men wanted a victory; an old enmity put away—a triumph over the Navajo.

Opening her stride, Rain began to pull from deep within the tension and tissue, the hurt and love that was herself, the power that was in her. At the same time, she fought the pain in her chest, the fire that burned her lungs as she ran. The face of her grandmother, the story of Born Of Water— these things kept flowing inside her, kept pushing her harder.

Now she was moving like her namesake. The hawk-wind rain. *I cannot be beaten in my own home,* she told herself. Running over the lava beds that The People called Blood of the Giant, she told herself, *slow down now, go a little easier. Going this hard could cost you the race. Listen to your heart, not your head. Run flat. Let your feet fall like drops of water. Wind-driven water.*

That's better. Feel the wind.

As soon as Rain said this to herself, she felt cold raindrops strike her forehead.

Good, this is the way I like it. With the hawk. The rain.

But she also felt the press of the men behind her. These were strong long-distance runners, mountain bred. They were not going to give up without a fight. She pushed harder on the ascent. And, somehow, knew they were gaining on her. One had even pulled out in front of the others. Her Navajo brother had fallen far behind; she couldn't feel his support any longer.

Now Rain saw the sky darken. Her face was lashed with tears, but there was no salt in them.

They were sky-fallen, and driven. She wet her dry lips with the rainwater.

The country changed again. They were out of the sage flats into the mesa lands. The trail was tightly carved out of the red clay ravines. Twice, Rain banged her elbows as she pumped upward, trying to gain speed on the incline. In her calves and quads, she experienced the onset of depletion. Once, she lost footing, staggered. It was just for a second, but when she bumped against the walls of the ravine, some dirt tumbled down the back of her singlet.

The country of the owl. Rain knew the land and the story well. How Born Of Water was taken in by Brother Owl. Hidden from enemies, made invisible. Otter Brother had taken him in too. And Brother Ground Squirrel. Rain laughed. She remembered how her grandmother used to change the animal genders to please her little granddaughter. The way the old stories were told, it was Brother instead of Sister. Grandmother made the animals into sisters.

The dark desert sky was shot with blue. Clouds, crimson and torn, dropped away. Out came the sun, white and hot. It burned the rainwater in the small of Rain's back where the dirt had fallen. She glanced up in the hope of seeing a hawk. But there was none. The empty vault of heaven had no message for her.

Rain ran on.

Ever more steep, the trail turned to a scarred floor of gleaming schist that twinkled in the sun. Now the sweat on her face mingled with the raindrops in her hair. Rain tasted two tastes on her tongue—salt and sweet.

Yet this pleasure lasted briefly. Rain's breath came in gulps. Shorter grabs of oxygen. And not enough of them. She dropped low, light in the knees. But gaining the top of the mesa was sapping her strength. She had no ready tricks for this steep, upward grind. The ascent itself was now her enemy; she thought no more of what was behind her.

She was, at last, in the place of no beginning and no end. She was moving on automatic impulse. Her body a thrusting, glowing machine of assembled parts that did what they did regardless of what she thought or said. Nor was she aware of the sleek dark runner who, during much of the race, occupied the position in back of her left elbow. He was the one she heard breathing. And now she seemed unaware that he had come out into the final stretch that led to the San Juan River. She saw the river, not the runner. *If I can just make that river. If I can make…*

A fine glitter of golden rain came from the cloudless dome of blue. The San Juan was the color of coffee mixed with cream, the edges white with froth. Minutes before the rainstorm, the cross-country ribbon sticks had fallen into the

river. Now they were gone. Nonetheless, the Ute man hit the water, full stride. He was a good length in front of Rain. A good head taller, too. Lean and rangy, he was gloating over his victory already.

But the truth was, Rain did not see him.

She felt her legs failing. She grit her teeth as the claws pierced her back, raising her high into the air.

Glancing upward, she saw the dark shroud of feathers. The hawk's head was high in the sky. She saw the point of its beak, glinting in the sun.

Its eye, orange. Below the San Juan churned like coffee milk. Rain thought she saw her feet dancing over the water, not really touching it except for a skimming motion, the way a hawk takes a trout on the wing.

Suddenly the fiercely sunk talons released Rain. She felt herself sprung, and free. A silvery spray came off her legs as she hit the gravel of the river. Her feet crunched. Then she was free and clear on the other side of the San Juan. The white strip of the winner's tape lay before her. Rain collapsed into it. *I feel the feathers brush my back,*

rise over my head. I am buffeted forwards. The
tips of the wings shear the air, go up, away from
the race.

The world darkened around her. Rain
dropped into that darkness. *The only thing left*
is my heart, my captured heart, still caught in my
chest. The rest of me is free.

Her loud heart hammered her awake. *My*
hawk sister circles the sun. Crying, I hear her cry.
She is telling me I have beaten that Ute warrior.
My grandmother and Born Of Water are proud.

All this, and fresh tears.

Another feather of rain. So that, she knew

She was Rain . . .

Rain.

Runner.

Dream Walkers

Jim Tom was sitting in English class listening to the teacher talk about plural nouns. His notebook was open and he was pretending to be interested in what she was saying, but his mind was elsewhere.

I'll give you plural nouns, Jim Tom said to himself.

He wrote the word cow fifty times in fifty different ways all over the blue-lined sheet of notebook paper.

Cows, plural. Cow, singular.

So simple any fool could get it. Then why did he—and half of his class—say corns, when they meant to say, corn?

Jim stared out the window. *The land is flat. Blues, grays, browns. Plurals. Different values of colored sand. Could you say sands? You could, couldn't you? What a funny language, English. I wonder if we think a certain way because of the words that we use—or don't use…I wonder if I'll ever speak good English. I wonder if I even want to.*

Jim's daydream took him far off into the backcountry of his mind. He went to places where his teacher with her grammar book would be completely lost. Places where he, Jim Tom, was completely at home.

Once, when I was five, my grandmother showed me the hogan where a witch was supposed to live. From that time on, whenever I saw that hogan, I thought about the witch. This was no woman on a broom with a cat. This was a man with great dark power. A man you left alone. When I was twelve, me and my brother Caleb saw the old witch man chopping wood. We crept up behind a big rock. We watched the man raise and lower the axe. We felt bad because that witch chopped wood just like anybody else. He breathed like other men, too. And he wiped the sweat off his face just like any other old man on the rez.

That guy looked normal in every way except for his hair, which was whiter than snow. Maybe he's no witch at all.

The next year Jim turned fifteen. Caleb was a year older. They were out on the mesa with the 22 rifle they shared and they were hunting ground squirrels. They stayed long into the afternoon. Around dusk, as they were getting ready to go home, a steer came bumbling out of the brush, and scared them. Caleb had the gun. Without thinking he raised it and fired. One bullet. And it went through the animal's left eye. The steer went down on its knees, rolled over on its side, and died. The sun was almost on the horizon. The wind whisked along the edge of the ridge.

"What do we do now?" Jim asked.

Caleb sighed. "Well, we can't let this meat go to waste."

"Are you saying we should butcher it?"

Caleb spat, wiped his mouth. "Let's do it fast."

"What for?" Jim asked. "It'll be dark soon. Who's going to see us?"

Caleb looked around the four directions. "Who knows," he said with a shrug.

They worked side-by-side using the sheath knives they carried with them when they went hunting. Caleb was the expert. Jim followed his

lead. It was a scrawny old steer, and not a lot of
meat. Caleb rigged up a sort of travois with the
blood-wet cow skin as the drag and two saplings
tied to the sides. In a couple hours they were
done. Both boys were spattered with blood. It
was on their clothes, hands, and faces. However,
in the dark they didn't know.

It took several trips off the mesa to get the
travois down. Meat kept spilling off the sides,
and they had to stumble around and find it. A lot
of it got lost in the dark. At last they were at the
base of the mesa with most of the meat.

"Now what do we do?" Jim said.

47

"We give it away," Caleb told him.

"How do we do that?"

"Watch me," Caleb said.

The brothers delivered chunks of beef on doorsteps in front of trailers, hogans and prefab houses around the area. Dragging the heavy load from house to house took some time. While they worked Jim was thinking. *Funny thing is, no dogs are barking. No doors are opening. It's like nobody knows we're out here. It's like the world's asleep. Like we're dream walkers.*

When the final load of meat was left on the metal stairs of a beat-up old trailer, Caleb turned to Jim, and said, "We made a mistake." They were walking home at a swift pace, and Caleb said this while looking back over his shoulder.

"Yeah. What mistake?"

"I just remembered the owner of that cow."

They walked in silence. Their boots made crunching noises on the short bunch grass.

Jim asked, "Was it the old witch?"

"Yeah."

"For real?"

Caleb didn't answer. They walked along more quietly.

"He's not a witch, anyway," Caleb said.

Jim didn't say anything.

They were nearing their home, when Jim said, "Grandma told me once that if you don't give a witch what's due, he can kill you." He snapped his fingers in the dark. "Just like that!"

Caleb snorted. "Just like that," he said softly. He was still carrying the bundle of wet cow skin. Suddenly, Caleb let it fall out like a blanket and draped it over his head and shoulders. He danced with the thing wrapped around him. The head of the cow bobbled up and down as if it were alive. Caleb's face, already stained, was really bloody now. Dripping with blood. He looked awful. Jim watched him shuffle about in the sand as if he were doing a little kid's version of a squaw dance. A thin morbid moon hung yellow and leering in the starless sky.

Caleb started up a little chant. "I'm gonna give the old man his due," he said at the end.

Finally, Caleb stopped fooling around. He was breathing heavy, sweating. Jim knew what Caleb was going to do.

"Don't do it," he warned his older brother.

Caleb snorted, and spat. His face was dark with blood. It was even on his teeth. The only white left on him was his eyeballs. All at once, Caleb took off, running. Jim followed after him. *I have nothing to do now but follow. I know it's wrong. Killing the cow was wrong. But this . . . this will get us into real trouble. Why am I not going home? Why am I following him?*

The hogan of the witch was close by. It was in a little valley surrounded by sand hills. The hogan was off to itself. To get to it, you had to walk down in plain sight of the hogan. There was

no place to hide. Just the hogan. The door to
the hogan, facing east. The burnt red dunes. The
night sky. The evil trickle moon.

Caleb went down the dunes to the hogan, as
if he didn't care. He walked proudly up to the
doorstep, holding the 22 rifle. Jim was a few steps
behind him, but he was not walking proudly. He
saw something that frightened him. A lightning-
struck tree. Bad sign.

In the thin light of the moon, Caleb mocked
the witch. He wore the blood skin of the cow and
he shook the rifle out in front of him like a staff.
But as he got to the door of the hogan, Caleb
stopped short. Gazing around, his shoulders sagged.
In that moment, he didn't look so sure of himself.
It was the isolation. The silence here was deep.

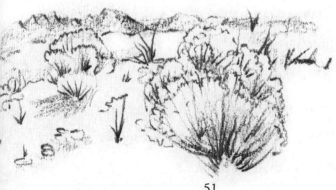

You could almost hear it. Then the wind came up like a crippled lizard. Little skittering noises came and went.

Caleb, hooded and hunched, seemed to be a statue. His blood-knuckled hand was out, extended for a knock that never happened.

What's he doing? It's like he's frozen. Caleb, get going! Drop the skin, let's get out of here! Whisper of juniper in the moon. No knock. Wind jitters. Stomach flutters. Nothing but night. So much night, so little of us.

Then Caleb broke free of whatever was holding him back.

His knock sounded so loud on Jim's ear. The echo followed the knock. But nothing happened. Then the door swung wide on a rawhide hinge. The darkness from within leaped out. The light from without leaped in.

All in silence.

Caleb gasped.

Jim jumped.

Then Caleb threw down the soaking skin.

Both boys ran for the dunes.

They ran through the dark wind.

In back of them, the hogan. Door ajar.

The wind, the dark.

The red diamond dunes.

The brothers ran without stopping. They took reedy breaths of air as they ran all out of breath, but they kept running for a good mile until they came to the ancient silver trailer with the hogan out back.

Jim, who was a faster runner than his brother, got to the standing pipe first. He knew what to do. Strip down fast, crank on the cold water. He rubbed himself with water and a handful of sand to get the matted blood off his skin. Then Caleb did the same. Jim shivered. Slipping on his blood damp shirt and jeans, he realized that his clothes smelled rotten with death.

Neither brother spoke of what they'd done. And whatever had happened back there at the witch house, that was sealed away. But now they knew they had to find a way into the trailer without disturbing their grandmother. She would be where she always was. In her favorite rocker in front of the TV.

There was no way in or out without being seen.

Jim thought, *Grandmother's waiting for us. Waiting like the moon waits on the hill for the first cry of a coyote. There's no getting out of this thing we are in.*

"We'll walk in and say nothing," Caleb said foolishly.

"That'll work," Jim said as sarcastically as he could.

"Quit that," Caleb said, shaking his wet hair.

"You quit that," Jim whispered.

They were both shivering, wondering what to do. Jim heard a distant ringing in his ear, like someone was calling him on the phone. He pressed his ear to make it stop.

"I feel dizzy," he told Caleb.

"Shut up, I'm thinking." Then he added, "OK. We just go in. That's all. We face her wrath. That's all."

"That's all?" Jim echoed.

Caleb swung open the trailer's screen door, then twisted the knob on the metal door, and stepped inside the warm small room. Jim followed. Their grandmother was in her rocker with a cotton Mexican shawl wrapped around her. The lights were off, the television was on. The inner walls of the trailer were trembling with reflections from the set. The sound was off, and the old woman was lightly snoring, her head fallen forward.

Jim and Caleb walked past her, single file.

The snoring stopped.

The boys stopped.

The snoring resumed.

The boys tiptoed into their bedroom.

Undressing in the dark, they got into bed without saying a word. They still slept in the bunk beds they'd had when they were little. Caleb on top, Jim on bottom. They were quiet for a while, then Caleb leaned his head down. "She never saw a thing."

"Want to bet?"

Jim didn't answer. Then, he said in a little whisper, "Did you see it?"

Jim said, "I saw it all right."

Somewhere off in the desert night, a dog howled. This was followed by a triplicate volley of coyotes. *The dog; the coyotes. The dog has a bigger voice, more high-toned. It's the preacher yelling at the choir. The coyotes are laughing at the dogs, mocking them, the way Caleb mocked the old witch...*

A long secret silence passed between the brothers. Then Caleb said, "I'm sorry Jim Tom."

"OK."

Caleb said, "If I hadn't of--"

"--If Grandmother had wheels, she'd be a bus," Jim broke in.

"Hey, I told you that one."

Jim asked, "Do you think..."

He didn't finish.

"What?" Caleb returned.

"Not so loud, bro."

"All right then—what?" Caleb whispered.

Each knew what Jim was trying to say, and

also why he didn't say it. Neither tried to start up again. They lay in their separate bunks, which were separate worlds, thinking to themselves. They had seen the face. Both of them. And it wasn't the face of a human being.

"I mustn't fall asleep," Jim said.

"Why mustn't you fall asleep?" the young teacher asked.

Jim opened his eyes, and realized he was in English class. He'd fallen asleep, in spite of telling himself not to, and now he'd embarrassed himself in front of everyone. He glanced about the room. "Where are the others?" he asked the teacher. She

was cleaning her round-rimmed glasses with a tissue paper.

"They're outside where you should be. It's lunch. Remember lunch?"

Jim rubbed his eyes. He could feel the woman's eyes taking him apart the way she took apart the English language, breaking the words up into little chips and lining them up on white paper. *I am not a sentence. I won't be broken up. Not by her anyway.* Jim stood up, and pushed his desk away from him.

"Where do you think you're going, young man?"

"Out," Jim said. "You said lunch."

He scooped up his books, and headed for the door.

Outside in the sunlight, he felt better. The air cleared his head. Jim looked at the long, low-lying shelves of desert sand. His home. The colored earth, slabs of burnt umber. Brown. Red. The red, his grandmother said, was blood. The blood of giants that once roamed the earth. Now, seeing it in the light of day, it was another kind of blood. The same kind he'd washed off his hands the night before.

Jim blinked in the noonday sun.

In front of his desert-dwelling eyes, he had a vision. Men and women tilling the soil, planting corn. They wore old-fashioned clothes. These were the Old Ones. He saw them so plainly, while, only seconds before there had been endless miles of desert. The Old Ones toiled in the sun. People from another time, but not another place. *I see them: their long black hair hanging down. They sing as they work. The song rises on the bright air and is part of the clouds. The spruces. The rocks. The corn. If I blink again, they will be gone.* He did so, and they vanished.

Then Jim went back to the school and sought his locker. He was smiling. Now he knew what to say to his brother.

That night when they went to bed, Jim wanted to tell his brother about the vision. How it presented itself to his eyes alone. How it vanished. He wanted to explain that this sort of seeing into time somehow cancelled the image at the witch's door. He wanted to say, *There is evil and there is good, and they live side by side, and they are brothers.* However, Jim kept quiet on all of it. Just before he fell asleep, he saw the door open

again. Inside the hogan, Jim saw the wolf. It was
sitting with paws folded. Then the face of the
wolf transformed into an owl. The owl lifted out
of the wolf and came out, claws spread. It came
for Caleb and Jim, and then it turned to vapor in
the air, and there was just the old man standing
there with his mouth open, breathing, coughing at
them with his voice of wind and dark that
followed them all the way home.

Now he lay in bed, thinking and not speaking.
Soon, he heard the deep, regular breathing of

Caleb as he slept on the bunk above. *Will I dream? Will I see the old man? Or the faces of the Old Ones? Will I cry out in my sleep?*

Jim Tom smiled. Once again, in that twilight world between sleep and wake, light and dark, he saw them.

I see the bodies coming up into the sun. Copper skin, long, black hair. I hear the sweet song of the earth in harmony with the Old Ones. The bright ears of the corn, singing. The men and women coming out of the earth. Like his own grandmother. Like the corn. Like the song the Old Ones were singing with the rising of the corn and the rising of the people.

This would keep him, this would protect him.

And the face of darkness had no dominion over his vision. That, he knew, was why the witch man lived alone. He had to stay in darkness in order to be what he was, what he had to be, to live.

His brother stirred, whimpered in his sleep.

"Don't worry," Jim said softly. "I am here with you."

Again, he saw the shifting rows of corn flashing in the sun. And he heard the song that made The People strong.

The sun, the earth, the song
The sun, the earth, the song

Jim whispered this over and over to his brother, who lay quiet and made no sound.

Crystal Wolf

he smell of honeysuckle came off the acacia trees and beckoned Mariah to pitch her tent. The air was full of the little wooly pills— blossoms of the acacia. Their fragrance drenched the air, and made it smell like heaven in the canyon. The camping spot was a dry place. Home of the red ant, the trapdoor spider and the alligator lizard.

Nearly noon and the sun was well above the canyon rim. The oven-like air was rose gold. Mariah put down the sketchbook with the drawing of a dragonfly. She walked to the river for a swim.

Close to the water, set like green lace, were clumps of watercress and wild celery. All around

the blue stream with its white sandy bottom were
bunches of cattails. Mariah edged into the water,
an inch at a time. Above her head in the white,
hot air catkins of cottonwood and ash rained
down, creating an illusion of little soap bubbles
glowing in the sunlight.

In the middle of the stream was a small island.
Mariah swam to it. In the center of the island, she
found a flat rock. On the top of it were four crystal
pebbles. The deliberate way the pebbles were
placed there told Mariah something. In a circle
like a snail shell they wound around. *Someone,*
she thought, *put these here. But for what reason?*

Thinking of the pebbles, she swam down-
stream. As she swam in the cold stream she
listened to the gargly song of the rain toads. They

were everywhere. It was mating season. Their
song was thick and dreamy, like the river itself. It
filled the woods with the clatter of life. Swimming
on her back, Mariah heard the toads, and smiled.
Looking up, she saw the catkins coming down.
This is a place where earth, water and sky meet.
A place where I am in the center of all things that
matter to me. I feel my soul expanding and
floating upward.

A little later while warming herself in the sun,
Mariah saw a dark-skinned Havasupai sawing a
log by the river. She greeted him with a soft hello.

The man nodded, but did not answer. He
was handsome, but his looks were dark as a canyon
shadow. He himself was in that shadow now,
sawing. Briefly, the two exchanged glances. His
was straight-to-the-heart. An unashamed stare that
seemed to go through her. *Maybe he is not looking*
at me at all, but rather at something behind me.

She looked at him tentative, and quick. Like
a swallow darting from a branch. Covering herself
with her towel, Mariah walked to the seeming
safety of her tent. Momentarily, she turned and
gazed again. He had a hard-boned muscular
face. Long, straight hair. And he was still looking

straight at her. Mariah went into the tent, and from within, looked out. To her surprise, the man wasn't there. The half-sawn log was there, gold and gray in the sun—but not the man.

That night after supper, Mariah thought about the day. The little island. The flat rock with the circle of pebbles. *I want to see it again. I must see it. I don't know why, but I must!*

She ran down to the stream and waded out into the chill water. All around her the rain toads roared with their mating song. The light of day was fading. The island was blue now, with the sun almost gone. The flat rock was there exactly as she'd seen it before. But now there were only two pebbles. She looked closely at them, but did not touch them. The pebbles were white quartz. They were touching each other, sitting in the very center of the stone. She drank in this strange sight, listening to the unraveling noise of the toads.

Back at her tent, Mariah put on a sweatshirt, and got into her sleeping bag. Soon she was comfortable. The canyon was still warm. In a little while Mariah felt hot inside the sleeping bag. She kicked herself free of it, opened the tent flap to let in the air. The night scents wafted into the enclosed space. She waited. Finally, a breeze brushed the leaves outside and cooled her skin. It was late when the air was cool enough to sleep. Mariah dozed on top of her bag.

And then, suddenly, she jumped out of her shallow sleep and stifled a scream with her fist.

The wolf was close to her face, silver eyes staring. A soft growl came from its parted lips. Mariah saw its teeth gleaming, then it swung about, neat and clean, and with one leap bounded out of the tent. Mariah heard soft paws on dry leaves. Pish pash, it entered the stream. Chumpf

chumpf, it arrived at the island, shook hindquarters and tail. Mariah watched as the wolf sniffed the two small pebbles. *I cannot see it but I can feel the pebbles moving. The night changing.*

For a long time, she stayed awake after this. Sometimes she heard noises, and was startled by them. Then, towards dawn, she fell asleep sitting cross-legged, her head angled to the side like a bird. It was midday when she woke covered with sweat. The tent was hotter than a bread oven. Mariah put on her bathing suit, pulled a t-shirt over it, and swam out to the island.

The flat rock was there, as she expected it to be.

But the pebbles were gone.

That day, crazy with heat and the calls of the canyon wrens, passed like any other.

A burning, honey-suckle scented, wild-celery-tainted afternoon. *The only thing missing is the toads. They're quiet. The canyon is still.*

Mariah listened for them. But they never started up. The woods seemed to want them. Yet they were nowhere to be seen. The canyon wrens carried the afternoon with their skirling, descending musical scales, but in time they too were silent. The canyon quiet was then as heavy as the heat of the previous day. *I wish the blue notes of the wrens would return. I wish the toads...I wish...I wish...what do I wish? Noise? Human action? The quiet has settled so deeply in the canyon that it presses upon my head, I can feel the weight of it on me like a burden.*

Feeling the stillness enter into her, Mariah gave into the canyon. She surrendered to a greater power of being. And, again, she waited. For what? She didn't know. For something.

Just before nightfall, Mariah filled her canteen at the stream. The sound of bubbles burbling was welcome to her ears. Evening was coming in the traditional way. The topmost walls of the canyon were still aglow. It was day up there in the higher country. The lower walls of the canyon were gray and gloomy. Night was forming in the pools under the grayish cliffs. Bats were squeaking. That song, too, Mariah welcomed.

As usual, she waded, then swam to the island.

The flat rock was in place.

But there were no pebbles.

That seems wrong. So flat. So empty. Did the wolf take the pebbles?

Mariah searched the base of the rock, feeling in the dusky light for the round quartz stones that weren't there.

Once in her tent, she vowed not to fall asleep. *I will wait for the wolf to come and I will not be asleep when it steps boldly in here.*

Why she didn't close the tent flaps and tie them, she couldn't have said; for she didn't know. And instead of staying awake, Mariah drifted off. When she awoke she was lying on her side, curled up in her sleeping bag. The tent was hot. The morning was half gone. The canyon was warming up for another blistering day.

Slipping on her bathing suit, Mariah cooled off. She dog-paddled out to the island. The rock was there, empty and bright. No pebbles. While swimming back to the tent to make breakfast, Mariah was certain of something. The idea came fast. *I am not wanted here. That's what the wolf was trying to tell me. I'm supposed to move my tent.*

By noon, Mariah packed and moved the tent to the east side of the river. There, sure she'd done the right thing, she spent the rest of the day nibbling raisins, sunflower seeds. She made a quesadilla: melted cheese, onion with a tortilla folded over it. A cup of river-cooled herbal tea for dessert. She spent the day idly drawing, feeling well fed and strangely secure.

In the early violet dusk, the heat was not oppressive and the night wind came early. Mariah

73

made a supper of mushrooms cooked with soy
sauce and butter and some pasta. A playful breeze
tickled her face as she cooked. The leaves of the
young ash trees along the canyon walls shivered.
The river sang. Mariah sat under the first stars,
and enjoyed the coming of night. She was leaning
against a back brace of woven saplings she'd made.
*I feel content. For the first time. I feel unafraid.
I feel I am who I am. I am not worried about
what will come.*

What came was the wolf.

It crept up to where she was sleeping against
the sapling brace.

Mariah woke; the wolf was sitting at her feet.

Its eyes were not angry.

She watched, barely breathing, wondering.

The wolf stood, stretched, yawned.

Then it padded to the river, went in, drinking as it walked.

Soon it was swimming to the island.

Mariah watched as the wolf did something with its nose.

She saw the white flag of its tail, wagging.

Then it was gone.

I feel it, the night change. It's come again, only this time it's different. The little engines of the rain toads have started. The noise is filling my ears and the cool air is flowing between the tree trunks.

Mariah sat still, listening to the changes. The canyon was brimming with grateful life. Things were moving, calling out to one another. A moment before it had been dead summer. Now, suddenly, it was spring, the way it should be, the way it was, for the month was May. The rain toads were joyous, ebullient, crazy. It was the time of the rain toads. Mariah fell asleep once more, just resting against her handmade chair of woven wood.

In the morning she couldn't wait to swim to the island. Such a feeling she had, the wonder of discovery. She was a child. It was Christmas for the first time. The toads and the wrens cheered her on as she swam. She knew little else than the joy of the morning. It was still early. The spell of newness hung like jeweled dew in the morning air.

On the island the flat rock was there.

The quartz pebbles made a perfect circle like the sun.

Mariah counted nine of them.

Seeing them, she named nine things that she loved:

The river, the toads, the wrens, the pebbles, the wolf, the trees, the sun, the canyon, and most of all, the morning.

The following day, Mariah loaded up her things, packed her backpack, and left on the trail that wound upward out of the canyon.

She stopped before noon at the village of Havasu. There she studied the community blackboard. The mule train had just come in with a week's worth of mail. The day was full of commotion. Dust and dogs. The canvas panniers of boxes from the world outside the canyon were taken off the mules by strong stout Havasu women. There was dust, dogs and white, wet mules. And confident women busy with their silent, thankful work.

I am watching how the women carry things. Each carton that goes into the tribal community center is sacred. They walk slowly in the heat of the day. The way they hold the box is gentle, like they're carrying a child in their arms. I am looking at one woman, and she is looking at me. I feel I would carry a box like a baby, too. But I have my backpack. That will be my baby as I carry it up out of the canyon into the light of the world.

Soon the village square was quiet. The peach trees along either side of the dusty road had green fruit. The children were playing in the shadows under the trees, using a hard green peach for a toy ball.

On the community bulletin board, Mariah saw a message scrawled in large letters:

WHITE PEOPLE WILL GIVE UP
DIGGING FOR URANIUM
WHEN MOTHER EARTH'S
HEART STOPS BEATING

Below this message was a wolf's paw print. The pads were red, green, gold and black.

Mariah studied the message and the symbol below it. When she was through the mule train was going up the trail ahead of her.

Time to go.   Time to leave my home.

On the way up the switchbacks leading out of the Grand Canyon, Mariah sang the song of going away, the song of leaving lovers and friends and all things of the natural world, toads as well as swallows, bats as well as ants.

As she went she sang the song of leaving.

The stars are the windows of flowers

Flowers are the windows of stones

I am the window of myself

And my pleasure is the gateway of the corn

Armed only with a song, she left the canyon.

Perhaps he will follow me, she thought.

But she knew he would not.

Zahgotah

hester Jim was a tracker. If you asked him what he liked to do more than anything else, he would say, "I like to track animals." And that was what he did, whenever he had a chance. But it wasn't how he made his living.

He earned his daily bread as a janitor at the Canyon Country Day School. Tracking animals was not profitable, so Chester did it as a hobby. Nevertheless, he was the best tracker on the Mescalero Reservation. Everyone knew he could find a hummingbird's nest in a summer sandstorm. Chester knew it too. So it didn't make much difference to him if he swept floors, washed boards, and emptied baskets for a living.

One weekend when he was packing some things in a knapsack and preparing to go off on one of his personal tracking expeditions, a man on a spotted horse rode up to his little shack.

The man was Lee Lazytree, a friend of Chester's from high school. Lee didn't bother to dismount. With the sun behind his head, long hair hanging down, shoulder-length, he looked like an Apache from a long time ago. The fact that Lee was wearing running shoes and a red baseball cap somehow didn't alter the image. Lee had a heavy face with small, narrow wolf eyes, and a long jaw. He was squat and heavy set.

"Goin' off?" Lee asked.

Chester tightened the straps on his old Boy Scout knapsack, a present from his father more than thirty years before. It looked new; the leather straps and the silver-alloy buckles were oiled and polished. Chester stuffed some elk jerky into the pack and hefted it easily to one shoulder. Then he looked into the quiet eyes of his friend.

Chester said nothing.

"Dry summer," Lee said, creaking forward a little in the saddle.

"Yeah," Chester said. "What you want, Lee? I'm on my way out."

"Wonder if you mind doin' us a favor."

From years of experience with his people, the questioning with eyes rather than words, Chester knew what was being asked of him. He also knew who was doing the asking. The Tribal Council was still out searching for Zahgotah, the man the people called "the enchanted Apache." No one could find him. Lee Lazytree had been delegated by the Council to give it another try.

"I don't know," Chester said hazily. "Zahgotah's been missing almost six months."

"His wife asked us to try one more time." Lee untangled his horse's mane from under the bridle strap that separated the horse's ears. A wasp made the horse sidestep just as Lee fingered the tangled mane. But Lee leaned with a graceful shift, as if nothing happened.

Chester smiled at his friend's agility. Chester was no horseman himself. However, he was, as his father once said, "from a line of old time Apache stalkers." These were men who prided themselves on footwork. Chester could walk all day and not

tire. All night, too, for that matter. And sleep standing up. Sometimes he slept standing just for the fun of it.

"—Well, what's it going to be, Ches?"

Chester squinted into the sun; he had less than a half-day of tracking left. Zahgotah was gone, but Chester wasn't going to say this to Lee because Lee knew it as well as he did. It wasn't worth saying. What the two men knew didn't need saying.

"I'll be talking to you," Chester said. Then he turned and headed toward the backcountry behind his shack.

"We'll be waitin' on you," Lee Lazytree said as Chester slipped into the cottonwood shadows.

As he walked along, feeling the hot sunlight on his shoulders and the good solid weight of the knapsack between his shoulders, Chester thought about the missing man named Zahgotah.

Chester remembered the morning, two months ago, when he was chasing a bear. He was studying the footprints in the mud. The back feet of a bear look like a man's shoeless feet with claws. The claws make a difference. Yet to Chester, it sometimes seemed he was tracking a man.

True, a bear and a man move in different ways. They have opposite styles of getting places. The man moves boldly, any which way. The bear though is cautious, curious. It's in the print—the way it meshes with the earth.

Chester remembered that October morning. The bear that day moved a bit too much like a man, he'd thought at the time. Then something happened.

The bear tracks turned into a man's. The man was wearing cowboy boots. There were four sets of prints. They crossed in and out. There were the bear's prints and then…nothing but the man's boot heels.

The boot heels wandered off a little ways, and faded out.

Chester gazed at the prints for an hour or more. He'd never seen anything quite like it. Finally, he accepted it, for what it was. Something that wasn't explainable. This was good enough for him. Good enough for government work, his friends used to say.

That's the way things were out in canyon country. *You didn't always have a ready explanation. Nor did you try to force one out of the mystery of life. You let it be. Went on with your business.*

However, some people saw the same thing Chester did. They made a fuss out of the bear-man prints. A hundred men on horseback saw what Chester saw. They said they knew the spirit that made the tracks.

Zahgotah.

The hundred men said they saw a whirlwind come up out of the sand and blow dust into their eyes. In the dust and wind, the men saw the shape of a man. The shadow of a man wearing white Tony Lama cowboy boots. When the wind let up, though, the man was gone. The only thing left was the white boots with silver tips. These were standing upright in the circle of baffled horsemen.

Nobody went near them.

Then the reverend over at White River said a sermon on that piece of work. "It's the Devil playing tricks. Trying to make bad men out of good men. I know some of you think it's Zahgotah. But that was a poor little man who was out of work. You know what that does to a man. All of you know that Zahgotah was an epileptic. He couldn't dance in a dust wind or

89

scale a cliff like a cat. Even though there's people that say they saw him do these things, we know better, don't we?"

Chester was at the sermon that day, and he smiled to himself. *What about the time in Badger Canyon. Some tribal policeman swore he saw Zahgotah dancing around on a cliff wearing those Tony Lamas that none of us wanted to touch. Jake Shonto claimed he saw Zahgotah dancing like a goat on the edge of a precipice.*

Jake and his friends were sitting around their campfire, talking and listening to gospel music. Someone said, 'Bet old Zahgotah would like to hear some of this music…too bad he's dead…' Then when Jake went to turn the radio up a little louder, he glanced up and there was Zahgotah dancing on a rim of rock. Looked just like a mountain goat. Some of the others said he looked like a coyote. One guy said Zahgotah's nose was longer than it'd ever been when he was alive. But it was him, everyone swore to that.

After that, everybody started seeing Zahgotah. There were people who saw him in Cibecue and Hon Dah on the same day. Those towns are far apart. But a man at a feed store in Cibecue swore

*he saw Zahgotah crouching over a spoiled grain
sack. He was eating rotten grain, the man said.
Stuffing it in his mouth, and swallowing it. Said
Zahgotah's shirtsleeves were trailing in the dirt.
His forearms all covered with long, dark-black
hair. Same day people over at Hon Dah claimed
Zahgotah was pitching horseshoes with some kids.
Said his teeth were little like a housecat's.*

Then the whole tribe went out on a massive
search and rescue. There were people who
believed that Zahgotah was alive; others didn't see
it that way. Chester thought back. *Well, what are
you going to do, if you find him? You can't arrest
a man for going away into the wilderness…you
can't put him into a hospital, if he doesn't want
to go…you can't send out a posse for a man who
hasn't broken any known law…*

Around that time there were lots of trackers
turning up every day looking for Zahgotah. It
got to be a regular off-season sport. A long hot
summer and no rain. Search parties fell all over
themselves. Hunters bragged about getting off
"sound shots" whenever something twitched in
the bushes.

No one knew what Zahgotah was living on—if, in fact, he was alive. A man can't live on one bag of spoiled grain. Some said he lived on juniper berries, wild grasses and chokecherry bark. Some said he ate raw deer meat, but they were the same trackers who said Zahgotah came to a dance one night in his white Tony Lamas. Danced the night to dawn—never missed a step. Some epileptic. Around sunrise a girl named Beverly Longbow went home and on the way she saw Zahgotah sitting by a large bear cub. She said, "That man and that bear were polishing his boots! The bear licked them with its tongue. Then Zahgotah rubbed the silver tips of the boots on the bear's neck fur to polish them."

Beatrice Zah, Zahgotah's widow, said this: "When I met him twenty years ago, the first words I ever heard him speak were—'I will be back tomorrow.' Now, he went away and didn't return for several years. He used to do this pretty regular. Then when he turned up missing this last time, I closed and locked my doors and windows. They told me he'd turned into something, and I got real scared."

Beatrice put holy oil on her front door every night. She brought out her Bible and blanket, and prayed for her husband's deliverance. One night she told some of her friends, "A mountain spirit came whispering around the house. The spirit told me not to worry, that my man, Zahgotah, was going to get found soon."

So, here was Chester Jim, out on his own remembering all these things while he was tracking the old bear-man once again. He was still only a few miles away from his shack when he came upon a young spruce tree. The score marks were the kind made by a bear cub, more playful than anything else. A happy cub having some fun. Chester sniffed the tear in the cotton flesh of the tree. It smelled of sweet wood, and bear.

And something more. Chester knew what it was. Leather polish.

Around at the back of the tree, there was a whitish thing.

Chester got down on his hands and knees.

Bones. White clean bones.

He sat down, got comfortable.

Not doing anything, he thought about Zahgotah.

People say he's a mountain spirit, a deer spirit, a goat spirit, a bear spirit. But I remember one time he threw down his Crown Dancer headdress in front of everyone. He stomped on it denouncing Apache religion. This was more than ten years before he started going away and turning into things. After throwing away his headdress, he joined the Miracle Church, the Spanish American Baptist Revival Church in White River. Zahgotah said, 'If I'm going to be cured of my illness, it's because Jesus Christ the Savior wants me to be cured, and not because some medicine man says a prayer with a pack of feathers.' Zahgotah was dead set against his people then, and he never really came out of feel-

ing that way. But after the Church revival stuff, he started going away. For longer and longer periods of time. Days, weeks, and finally months. When he'd return there'd be a strange light in his eyes.

Maybe Zahgotah got snake bit.

Maybe he didn't.

Maybe he went back to the hills to reclaim whatever he lost when he went to Vietnam. He never spoke about that.

Maybe, maybe, maybe.

But people say he turned into something.

Maybe he did, at that.

Maybe what he turned into wasn't as bad as people thought.

Maybe they were all a little jealous of him.

Chester sat beside the spruce tree for quite a long time. He opened up his knapsack. There was a thermos and he took a long pull on the hot coffee. Then he took off his hiking boots and socks. Chester lay back, barefoot, staring into the spruce boughs.

There was something up there.

It was white. And it was moving in the wind.

Chester hardly moved at all.

He lay there on his back, staring straight up.

Finally, he figured what it was.

Hanging on a deer hide thong was a pair of Tony Lamas.

Same time he saw them, Chester remembered Zahgotah's American given name. *It's funny, that name. Because like a lot of things that didn't belong—the Miracle Church, the unemployment, the work that Apache people did because no other work was available, families not getting along and always the young ones going off to the cities where they found trouble more easily than work—the name, the names, the American given names didn't ever belong.*

I guess that Zahgotah's one of the rare few who've beaten the rap. Confused just about everyone. In the process, lost his American given name. No one would ever call him Humphrey again. People even stopped calling him Zahgotah, for that matter. After the papers called him 'the Enchanted Apache' other people did, too. No doubt, he's a legend. And I'm the only one who knows whether he's dead or alive.

Pale Ghost

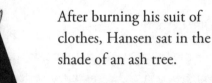After burning his suit of clothes, Hansen sat in the shade of an ash tree.

Soon the ghosts would come. They always did.

The sweat lodge, made of mud and stone, was so hot when he stepped into it; it singed the hairs inside his nose when he tried to breathe. *How do the old people do this?* The sweat flowed in rivulets down his chest.

> *City-bred skin*
> *Soft city hands*
> *City city man*

Hansen tapped the lava rocks with the deer antlers, moving them into place. Then he pulled the old blanket over the doorway. Immediately he was swallowed up in darkness, and the sweat of his steaming body ran into the dirt.

Prepare the place for the ghosts and they will come . . .

Hansen went outside for the third time, walked into the river, rolling like a dog in the shallows, sending minnows flying in all directions.

One more time.

For the fourth and final time, he pulled the blanket. The daylight was again sealed from him. He was in the womb of time, bathing his skin in the old life, birthing himself in the original wetness of being.

The ghosts, the parts of himself that kept him alive . . .

. . . Not there but soon . . .

The sweat rolled from his cheeks, collecting in pools around his navel.

For some reason he remembered his grandfather.

Perhaps it was the antlers. Remembering his grandfather made him remember his grandfather's tractor, the first one ever brought into the canyon.

That was years ago before Hansen was born. *They brought it in on mule back, one piece at a time. The elders thought it would ruin the way things were. But it made things better. The peaches could be harvested more easily, the earth furrowed faster. After a while everyone used the tractor. I saw it just the other day. Rusted out with datura blossoms like moons growing out of the rotten tires.*

When the thing first broke down, Grandfather
put a deer skull into the hub of one of the wheels.
When it broke down for the last time, Grandfather
was already in the ground and I was on my way
to government school in Lawrence, Kansas. Me
and my brother put the deer skull back in the hub.
That skull still had the bullet hole that had
killed the deer. We painted a portrait of
Bob Marley on the skull and the hole where the
bullet went through was the singer's open mouth.

Now, nine years later, all of them were in the
earth—the deer, the grandfather, the brother, the
tractor, the singer.

Soon they would come to soothe him . . .

He sang the old songs of thanks then . . .

Song to the roundness of things.

Song to the beaten bracelet, the sun-shaped
basket, the moon-shaped basket, the lodge made
of earth, the cedar trunk, the river that would
round the earth, the stars that embraced all of
them. He sang the song of first-breath, the song
the river makes in the new morning when the sun
is first-seen, first-felt.

Then he threw back the blanket . . .

. . . Ghosts . . .

The river cooled his hot skin. He rolled in the shadows for the last time. He came out of the cold into the hour of deception, just before evening, when shadows are born. The time when warriors strike upon the unwary. The time when the eye is not sharp. The time when things are not separate. The lost time when things are tied together. The time when one thing becomes another.

Hansen stood there in the cracking starlight and he knew that the cracks were crickets.

Crickets and stars.

Stars and crickets.

Cri, cri, cri. Str, str, str.

Cristr, crstr, crstr.

Then, listening, Hansen remembered his grandfather tell the tale of how, when he was a young boy, he ran 150 miles to see the train pull into the town of Williams. He hadn't stopped; he'd run the whole way.

The language, the old words, came back to him now in clicks and clacks like the song of the cricket stars. The language of ghosts.   He stood

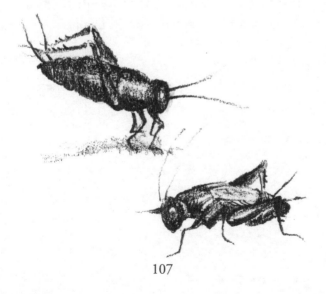

by the river, dry. Hot as an ear of roasted corn, dry and songless, trying to remember more, trying to squeeze the fruits of memory.

The words were like flat rocks rubbed together and they were like the rushes of yucca plaited one-over, one-under, until, miracle—there was a basket. Words, he thought, were like this.

Ghosts . . .

At first he thought it was a cloud of pollen on the wind.

Grandfather?

Allen?

Tractor?

Deer?

But the ghost was all of these, a thing of permanent parts, like the tractor itself, brought in, piecemeal on mule back.

Hansen saw, quite distinctly, his grandfather. He was made of the blue pollen that rests on ponds. Out of his body came the tractor, the way it looked when it was new. And sitting on the big metal seat shaped like a leaf was his brother Allen, the way he looked when he was alive, before he took his life, jumping off the cliff. And the deer, bounding like a legend, sprang out of Allen's mouth.

Going down on his knees, Hansen cried.

He cried for the missing parts, for the parts that rust in the sun and rain, for the bones that do not stay, for the people that blow away.

Lastly, he cried for himself.

When he stopped crying, he looked up.

Allen was there, his skin like shining pollen.

"I have loved you like a living brother," he said.

"You are my brother, aren't you?" Hansen asked.

"Yes," Allen said. "I will always be your brother." After a pause, Allen asked, "Have you called on me to tell you something?"

"Yes," Hansen cried. "What shall I do?"

"What shall you do? What you always do. That is what I have been saying all these years."

Hansen still looked uncertain.

Allen laughed, gently.

When he stopped laughing, Allen was Allen again. He looked very real to Hansen. Not pollen-like. Real. A man of flesh and bone.

"You--"

"Yes," Allen said. "It is what I have been saying to you all these years."

"—Are the one who is alive!"

It was Hansen, then, who dissolved, his face full of surprise.

The meeting done, Allen walked back to the village where his grandfather was waiting for him.

He was one with his brother for another year.

Notes on the Stories

Little Bear Canyon

I was in the Gila Wilderness camping in the canyon called Little Bear. Loren was there and my daughter Mariah and a number of my students and this was our year-end trip. The canyon was haunted and we felt the presence of spirits that lived there, spirits from long ago.

Loren went out by himself one night and got lost. Mariah was staring at the full moon. She said, "Something's happened to Loren." A while after this he came into camp very early, or very late, and told us of the small man he called Watcher.

A few days later I went on a climbing trip and found the little hidden house of stone described in the story. From the moment I entered that private silence, I felt the canyon ghosts press in on me. I felt Watcher and his family. He was almost visible but not if you looked directly at him. What you saw was a shadow; a "shade" they say in the old ghost books.

Loren saw him. Harry saw him. Jeff, the most reasonable member of our group, said he saw him.

I believe he must've been a tough little Mimbres man caught in a crack of rock that was stuck between the worlds. A spirit of the past living in the present, and remembering what he'd forgotten to do, living and re-living his responsibilities. As they say in Buddhism, if you don't get it right in the first world, you must try again.

Rain Runner

In the fall of 1988 I was writing an article on the Native American cross-country running team, Wings of the Southwest. I toured the country from the Hopi mesas to the North Carolina woods, and I wrote what I saw and Rain Runner was a part of that writing and running.

Rain Runner ran for her tribe. The willingness to run for the spirit of the event rather than for any kind of personal reason moved me when I spoke to her. She said that she was not merely one, but one of many. From this came her strength of vision, her strength as a runner. She didn't see herself winning; she saw herself running. So she wasn't alone when she raced. She was with her people; they were with her. The rich mythology of clan and kin comes up in the story. It tells of Navajo origins and speaks of gods that give aid to those who deserve help. Rain Runner finds her moment, too. She's helped by a spirit who lifts her over the edge of exhaustion and carries her across the river. There is an old Navajo story about this same thing happening to one of the sons of the Sun Father who is being chased by a Ute raiding party.

115

Dream Walkers

The background of Dream Walkers came from
members of the Native American resistance
organization, A.I.M. Two Navajos shared their
story of a personal rite of passage. How they
killed a cow, met a witch, and then paid the price
for stepping over the line. That was how they
described it—to them it was a moral dilemma.
Yet they made sure I understood there is a place
on the earth where evil happens; where the earth
itself is cursed by some ancient, awful, long-
forgotten historical event.

The story also deals with two brothers who
seem much like the Navajo Hero Twins. They
are characters of human destiny as well as ancient
gods. One of them is bold and swift. He is a warrior. His brother, though, is soft and reflective.
Perhaps he's less warrior than thinker, but he's no
less dynamic, in terms of grace and power. And
some say he is the clever one of the two, and often
the one whose moral choices save him.

Sons of the Sun Father. Together they are like
two aspects of humanity--active and inactive. And
they are dependent upon one another, because

thought without action is usually ineffectual. While action without thought is often an exercise in failure. Caleb Tom is like a dangerous strike of lightning--remember the lightning-struck tree in the story? Jim Tom, his brother, is like the sun on the water, bright and reflective.

My old Navajo collaborator and thirty-year friend Jay DeGroat dropped by to see me when I was writing this story. He told me he'd just had a vision of the old ones bending like the corn. He went on to say that the old ones were the corn. Jay said that when, as a Navajo, he truly understood his place on the earth as being of the earth, then he became, at that moment, one of The People. This is the spiritual blessing of Jim Tom and he confers it upon his older, but not wiser, brother, Caleb. We come from the earth and to the earth we shall return. There is no evil under the sun when we know our place and stay within its sacred, unbroken circle.

Crystal Wolf

A Pueblo friend of ours did not permit his daughter to go to Havasu in the Grand Canyon unless she was with a family member or a medicine man of Santo Domingo. There are places of such strong spirit, and in them spirits dwell. Havasu is such a place.

It is a strange and magnificent place, a side canyon that dwarfs all things human. And yet, at the same time, it brings the human and the supernatural into balance.

Visitors to Havasu sometimes tell of hearing voices lifted on the wind-currents. They hear lonely cries in the blue braids of the waterfalls. They hear voices that croak in lost tongues, lost languages.

Campers who stay in this part of the canyon talk of eerie feelings when they visit the Havasupai cemetery. Maybe they shouldn't be, but they are—and they see and hear things, so they say. I have talked to them. Sometimes climbers striking out for the high red walls above the cemetery turn back, for no reason. They say something tells them, "Go home."

A back-packer I met while camping at Havasu one summer, said, "I heard a voice while I was swimming underwater. The voice said, 'Go back.' So I did."

One night I woke and stood upright before my tent speaking in tongues. I was gesturing with my hands and though my eyes were open, I saw nothing, for I was still asleep. I appeared to speak to someone who wasn't there. My close friend, Ray Griffin, saw me standing in the moonlight, whispering and gesturing. He said I talked in a language that had repetitive sounds that came from deep in the throat. It was like nothing he'd ever heard before. "What did it sound like?" I asked him. He said, "It sounded like Tewa, maybe. No, it sounded like...Anasazi?"

"No one's ever heard that," I said.

He laughed. "I did."

The story of Mariah and the wolf happened pretty much as described in the story. The incident of the wolf entering the tent happened to me, personally. But whether the wolf was a dream animal—a spirit projection of a dreamer—I don't know. I do know that when I awoke, it was still there, and I thought it was a real wolf because it surely looked like one. I was startled into wakefulness, and when I saw the wolf at the opening of the tent, I told it to go away. At that same moment, I heard voices. I got out of the tent and saw someone running off into the darkness. Which brings me back to our Pueblo friend who forbade his daughter to stay where we were camped. Spirits and the people who dream them into our heads are real, more often than they're imagined, especially at Havasu, I think.

Zahgotah

My brother Sid, the artist who did the drawings
for this book, told me about Zahgotah. He heard
about him on one of his folk singing road trips.
For years Sid and I have been swapping stories of
Navajo witches and werewolves, Pueblo clowns
and Apache demons. The old ways, "the supersti-
tions" as they're sometimes called are being casu-
ally cast off by logic, reason and the determination
of some to eradicate the ghosts of the past. The
Zahgotahs of our world are disappearing because
we do not want to believe in them anymore. Or
possibly we have no need of them. With the
going away of legends, we, as a collective human
culture, are somehow less for our loss of belief.

Somehow, the Zahgotah myth, or reality,
fought its way into the open. It wouldn't go away.
Originally told as fact—even though it sounded
like fiction—the story proved that the human
spirit is unquenchable.

What made me wonder about the story and
the way people told it was their weaving together
of Christian and non-Christian folklore.
Zahgotah was a martyr of the old ways. After he
surrendered himself to the spirit world of the

animals, after he'd cut off his ties with the church and his people, he began to find a following—not that he wanted it, he didn't. Zahgotah became a kind of mystic messenger, someone like the prophet Wovoka or Handsome Lake. Zahgotah's message was that the old ways are alive and well, and no one can stop them.

After a while, nobody knew if Zahgotah was a man of flesh or one of spirit. But almost everyone agreed that he was a man of principle, not a crazy person. He knew the way back into the spirit world and he could come and go as he pleased. He expected no converts. In writing this story, I became one.

Pale Ghost

This story was told to me by a friend at Havasu. He talked about a spirit woman who wore her hair and clothes in the old style and who went about offering a basket of blue corn to campers. The way my friend told it the lady was not a ghost. "Ghosts are what old people use to scare young people," he told me. "This woman comes from some other place. On occasion you can see her. That's all." I took this to mean that she lived in another dimension, but that sometimes the worlds, as it were, collide, and we can see into them. I asked, "Have you seen her?" He smiled, said no. "The reason is that I want to see her. But she only comes to those who don't care to see her."

"Who has seen her then?" I questioned.

"The only people who see her are tourists who think she's a woman from our village." He paused and watched the wind in the trees moved by the air stream of the upper canyon.

"Is she?"

"She was—hundreds of years ago."

I thought about what was said, and it occurred

to me that the word ghosts is a misnomer.
That is why it's not used very much by Indians.
Depends upon the tribe, of course; Navajos use it
to describe things that are evil sometimes. Pueblo
people don't talk about ghosts. They say, when
someone dies, that he's gone. Not dead, just gone.
The word spirit came up often enough at Havasu.
One man I talked with said, "It's foolish to isolate
a spirit and call it a ghost. All things, dead and
alive, as you would say, have spirit in them; and so
they are all possessed of spirit."

At Havasu the gentle winds change with the
fiery or muted colors of the cliffs that turn saffron
at eventide, then plum and dark blue, and finally
black with the fall of night. The moon comes out,
and things turn again. As morning comes the
colors begin again. It's not ghosts but the mood
and spirit of all life is in the canyon and color is a
spirit there.

There is no time in the canyon except that
which you bring with you or that which is marked
by sun and moon, wind and shadow. If you bring
ghosts, they'll sit at your campfire and tell you
things. If you don't, they'll present themselves as
spirits. In any case, you have the colors.

About the Author

Gerald Hausman is the author of *Turtle Dream,* which is also illustrated by his brother, Sid Hausman. His other Native American books include *The Story of Blue Elk,* illustrated by Kristina Rodanas and *The Coyote Bead.*

About the Illustrator

Sid Hausman, folksinger, songwriter and illustrator is the creator of *One Bullfrog* and *Cactus Critter Bash,* both published by Azro Press. His CDs and performances are well known to listeners throughout the West.

Books of related interest by Gerald Hausman

Turtle Dream

The Coyote Bead

The Story of Blue Elk

Prayer to the Great Mystery: The Uncollected Writings and Photography of Edward S. Curtis

By Sid Hausman

One Bullfrog

Cactus Critter Bash